Dear Parent:
Your child's love of reading starts here!

Every child learns to read in a different way and at his or her own speed. Some go back and forth between reading levels and read favorite books again and again. Others read through each level in order. You can help your young reader improve and become more confident by encouraging his or her own interests and abilities. From books your child reads with you to the first books he or she reads alone, there are I Can Read Books for every stage of reading:

SHARED READING
Basic language, word repetition, and whimsical illustrations, ideal for sharing with your emergent reader

BEGINNING READING
Short sentences, familiar words, and simple concepts for children eager to read on their own

READING WITH HELP
Engaging stories, longer sentences, and language play for developing readers

READING ALONE
Complex plots, challenging vocabulary, and high-interest topics for the independent reader

ADVANCED READING
Short paragraphs, chapters, and exciting themes for the perfect bridge to chapter books

I Can Read Books have introduced children to the joy of reading since 1957. Featuring award-winning authors and illustrators and a fabulous cast of beloved characters, I Can Read Books set the standard for beginning readers.

A lifetime of discovery begins with the magical words **"I Can Read!"**

Visit www.icanread.com for information
on enriching your child's reading experience.

For Zoe Anastas with a big hug
—J.O'C.

For the fine illustrators in Owen Anastas's
second-grade class at Colonial Elementary
School who contributed to this book
—R.P.G.

For the Gardener Gang, who knows that
picking wildflowers is worth risking the itching
—T.E.

Fancy Nancy: Poison Ivy Expert Text copyright © 2009 by Jane O'Connor Illustrations copyright © 2009 by Robin Preiss Glasser All rights reserved. Manufactured in China. No part of this book may be used or reproduced in any manner whatsoever without written permission except in the case of brief quotations embodied in critical articles and reviews. For information address HarperCollins Children's Books, a division of HarperCollins Publishers, 195 Broadway, New York, NY 10007. www.icanread.com

Library of Congress Cataloging-in-Publication Data
O'Connor, Jane.
  Poison ivy expert / by Jane O'Connor ; cover illustration by Robin Preiss Glasser ; interior illustrations by Ted Enik. — 1st ed.
    p. cm. — (Fancy Nancy) (I can read! Level 1)
  Summary: A young girl who uses fancy words and considers herself practically a poison ivy expert learns a valuable (and itchy) lesson about the plant after picking a bouquet of wildflowers.
  ISBN 978-0-06-123614-3 (trade bdg.) — ISBN 978-0-06-123613-6 (pbk.)
  [1. Poison ivy—Fiction.] I. Preiss-Glasser, Robin, ill. II. Enik, Ted, ill. III. Title.
PZ7.O222Fgm 2009   2008013859
[E]—dc22   CIP
                                                                                                                    AC

17 18 SCP 10 9 8   ❖   First Edition

I Can Read!

BEGINNING READING **1**

Fancy **NANCY**

Poison Ivy Expert

WITHDRAWN

by Jane O'Connor

cover illustration by Robin Preiss Glasser

interior illustrations by Ted Enik

HarperCollinsPublishers

Look!

I am picking

a bouquet of wildflowers.

(Bouquet is fancy

for a bunch of flowers.)

"Watch out for poison ivy,"

Mom keeps warning me.

"I am! I am!" I say.

I know what poison ivy looks like.

I know the rhyme.

"Leaves of three. Let it be."

Why, I am practically

a poison ivy expert.

The next day

I bring the bouquet to school.

Bree brings cupcakes.

Robert brings purple punch.

We conceal everything.

(Conceal is a fancy word for hide.)

We are having a surprise party

for Ms. Glass.

It is her birthday!

By lunchtime

I am so excited about the surprise

that I get all itchy.

My arms itch.

My nose itches.

Every inch of me itches!

"Nancy, you have red bumps
on your face," Bree says.

I do?

Yes! I do!

Ms. Glass calls home.

Dad picks me up

and we go to the doctor.

Can you guess what is wrong?

Yes! I have poison ivy.

It is all my fault!

I am not a poison ivy expert
after all.

And what if my bouquet
had poison ivy in it?

Dad lets me call Ms. Glass.

"There is no poison ivy,"

she tells me.

"Just beautiful flowers.

Merci, Nancy."

(Ms. Glass knows I love French.)

She hopes I am better soon.

Later, Bree stops by.

I am too itchy for company.

So she sends stuff over

in our mail basket.

A note from Ms. Glass says,

"Everyone is starting a journal.

You can write yours at home."

Bree's note says,

"Thursday is Picture Day.

Will you be back?"

No, I won't be back Thursday!

I am miserable.

(That's even worse than unhappy,

and also much fancier.)

All night I itch and itch.

The next morning

I am exhausted.

That is fancy for very, very tired.

Mom shows me a little jar.

It is from the lady next door.

"Mrs. DeVine says to put
this cream on your bumps,"
Mom tells me.
"It is a home remedy."
A remedy is fancy for medicine.

Ooh la la! I don't itch.

What is this magic cream?

Mrs. DeVine says

it has jewelweed in it.

Jewelweed grows in her garden.

I like the name!

Weeds are not fancy.

But jewelweed sure sounds fancy!

Mom brings home a library book.

I learn about poison ivy.

Then I start my journal.

I put in many fascinating facts.

(Fascinating is fancy

for interesting.)

In the fall, poison ivy turns red.
It looks very beautiful.
But don't let that fool you.
Stay away!

summer

fall

Dogs are lucky.
If they touch poison ivy,
nothing happens to them.

My dog, Frenchy

If you touch a person
with poison ivy,
you will NOT catch it.
Just don't touch clothes
that still have poison ivy on them.

By Sunday

I really am a poison ivy expert.

Tomorrow I go back to school.

Yippee!

In the afternoon
I go to Bree's house.

Ooh la la!

There is a surprise party,

for me!

There are cookies and punch.

And we all dance

to an old rock and roll song.

Guess what it's called?

"Poison Ivy."

Fancy Nancy's Fancy Words

These are the fancy words in this book:

Bouquet—a bunch of flowers

Conceal—hide

Exhausted—very, very tired

Fascinating—interesting

Merci—"thank you" in French (you say it like this: mair-SEE)

Miserable—very unhappy

Remedy—medicine